This book belongs to

Hi my name is

DICKiNSON

For Dave, and Roxy dog.

ISBN 978-1-84135-913-7

First published 2012

Published by Award Publications Limited,
The Old Riding School, The Welbeck Estate,
Worksop, Nottinghamshire, S80 3LR

www.awardpublications.co.uk

13 2

Printed in China

Also available:

Goose
Goose Goes to School
Happy Birthday, Goose!
Goose on the Farm
Goose Goes Shopping

Goose Goes to the Zoo

by Laura Wall

AWARD PUBLICATIONS LIMITED

Sophie and Goose are best friends.

They do everything together.

But there are some things that
Sophie and Goose can't do together.

Sophie can't fly.

She's not fond of goose food, either.

And when Sophie goes to school,
Goose has to stay at home.

Sophie worries that Goose is lonely when she is at school.

Perhaps Goose needs another
friend to play with, too?

Sophie wonders where she
can find a friend for Goose.

Then she has a marvelous idea. The zoo!

There are all sorts of strange noises
coming from inside the zoo.

But Goose isn't scared.

So together they go through the gates ...

... and into the zoo.

Sophie finds a big spotty giraffe.

He seems nice and friendly, but he can't fly.

No matter how hard they try.

Goose sees a smiling crocodile in the pool.

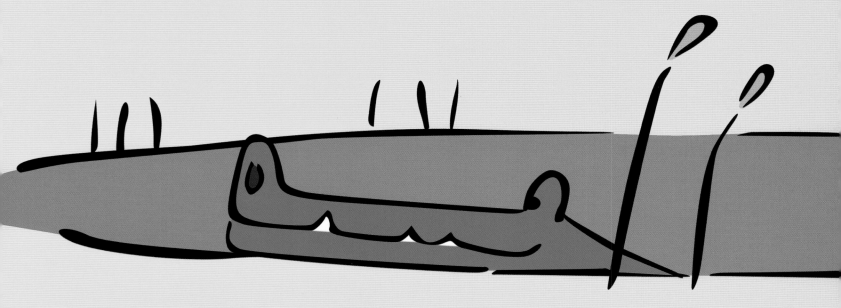

Perhaps he could be Goose's new friend.

But he likes the wrong sort of goose food!

Sophie and Goose find some pink birds.

But they don't seem to do much!

Oh dear. Poor Goose.

Then, Sophie and Goose hear
a familiar sound.

Honk!
honk!

honk
Honk!

honk
Honk!

Honk!
honk!
honk

honk

honk
Honk!

honk

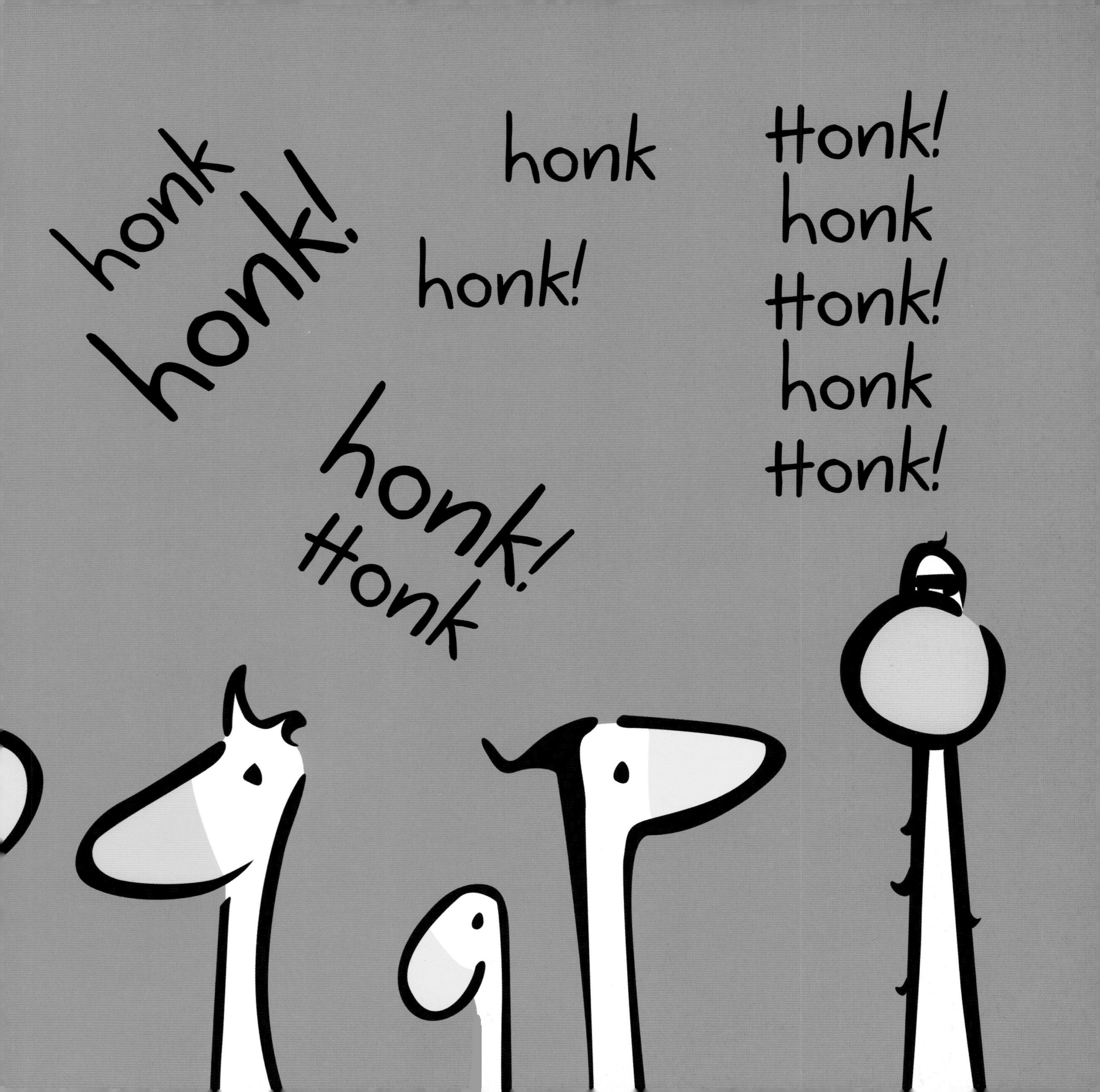
honk
honk!
honk
honk!
honk!
Honk
Honk!
honk
Honk!
honk
Honk!

"Look! Lots of geese, just like you!"

They ask Goose to go and fly with them.

And they share a snack.

They seem like very good company.

Sophie's glad Goose has found some new friends to play with.

She is happy for Goose.

Really, she is.

And Goose likes his new friends, too.

But there's no friend quite like Sophie.